Porky Pig and Bugs Bunny
Just Like Magic!

by Stella Williams Nathan

illustrated by Bob Totten and Tom McKimson

GOLDEN PRESS • NEW YORK
Western Publishing Company, Inc., Racine, Wisconsin

NOPQRST

Porky Pig looked worried.

"Bugs, we've been all over town," he said. "We've
got to find jobs, because today is Petunia's birthday.
How will I be able to buy her a present?"

Bugs scratched one long ear and pointed down the road. "How about working at that country place over there?" he suggested. "Looks like it's got a terrific vegetable garden. See the lettuce, radishes, green beans, and—wow!—*carrots* growing in that garden!"

Down the road they went, and Porky rang the doorbell. A tall, thin man opened the door.

"Good morning, sir. My name is Porky Pig, and this is my friend Bugs Bunny. We are two willing workers looking for a job."

"That's right, doc!" Bugs said eagerly. "We figured this place could really stand a good cleaning up."

The tall, thin man looked doubtful. "Well, I could
use some help, but I—" He stopped short, then went
on. "Come on in. There's certainly plenty to do."
And he brought out mops, brooms, dusters, pails,
soaps, and cleansers. "My name is Mortimer," he said.
"I'll be in to check on you later."

Porky started to dust all the furniture. Bugs was mopping, slowly and dreamily, when he knocked over the pail, and water spilled all over the floor. With a sigh, Porky mopped up the spilled water.

"Why don't you dust, Bugs?" asked Porky. "You can't get in as much trouble that way."

Bugs started to dust a table. Suddenly there was a loud crash. The table had collapsed to the floor.

Bugs jumped back in alarm. "Hey, what's up, doc?" he demanded. "This is pretty spooky furniture Mortimer's got here!"

Porky shook his head. "Come on, Bugs. I'll put it together," he said. "Nothing seems to be broken. You take the silver polish and work on shining up that suit of armor. You *can't* hurt that . . . I hope!"

As Bugs polished the armor, the visor fell down with a loud clang. Bugs raised the visor and took a look inside.

"Look, Porky!" he shouted as he brought out a large handkerchief from inside the helmet. He waved it at Porky, and the handkerchief turned into a bouquet of flowers. Then four pigeons flew out of the helmet, and one of them perched cheerily on top of Bugs's head.

Bugs turned pale. "Hey, what goes on?" he gasped.

Suddenly Porky began to laugh. "I think I know, Bugs," he chuckled. "I think we're cleaning a magician's house! *He'd* use pigeons in his *act!*"

"You're right!" Bugs looked very relieved. "That breakaway table, that bouquet of flowers, those pigeons flying out of that suit of armor! Of course! I knew it all the time, Porky."

Then Bugs stretched out on the huge sofa. "I don't know about you, Porky, but cleaning spooky magicians' houses wears me out."

"Are there *any* kinds of houses that don't tire you out, Bugs?" asked Porky.

Just then Mr. Mortimer entered the room. "I doubt
it, Porky," he commented. "Just resting, eh, Bugs?"
He looked around. "Well, you two have certainly
worked hard. At least, *one* of you has worked hard."

Mr. Mortimer hesitated. "I'm ashamed to tell you this, but I don't have enough money to pay you properly. Is there—is there something I can do to reward you for all your hard work?"

"Well, of all the nerve! And after I've worked till I'm exhausted!" said Bugs.

"What did you have in mind, sir?" asked Porky, after shushing Bugs.

"Well," Mr. Mortimer said shyly, "I'm Mortimer the Marvelous, and if I do say so, I'm terrific! May I put on a show for you?"

Porky was thrilled. "That's a wonderful idea, Mr. Mortimer! I'll invite my friend Petunia, too, as a special birthday treat."

"Just a minute," said Bugs. "None of that magician show stuff for me. After all my hard work, I deserve a bushel of carrots, at least!"

"I'm not so sure you worked all that hard, Bugs," Mr. Mortimer said, a bit scornfully. "But I'll make a bargain. If you'll act as my special assistant during the magic show for Porky and Petunia, I'll give you your bushel of carrots."

And that was how it happened that, later that evening, Mortimer the Marvelous reached into a hat
and pulled out—a surprised Bugs! Porky and Petunia
laughed and clapped.

Mr. Mortimer helped Bugs climb into a large trunk, then closed the lid.

"What's up, doc?" asked Bugs—and a moment later he crashed through a trapdoor. Porky and Petunia clapped again as Mr. Mortimer opened the trunk and showed them it was empty.

A moment later, Bugs came limping back into the room, and the magician told him to lie on a table.

"Rise . . . rise, Bugs," he chanted, waving his hands. Suddenly Bugs felt himself floating in the air, as light as a feather.

"No, no! Help! Help!" shouted Bugs. "Let me down! Please let me down!"

Mr. Mortimer clapped his hands sharply, and Bugs fell to the floor with a crash. "Delighted to be of help, old boy," murmured the magician.

Later, Bugs, looking weary and sore, complained as he carried home the bushel of carrots he had earned. "Boy, am I tired!" he exclaimed. "I haven't worked that hard in ages. That magician was really hard on me with all those tricks!"

"I thought he was a very nice fellow," Porky said happily. "And look at the wonderful present I have up my sleeve. He said it's for you, Petunia."

Porky brought out a long, brightly colored scarf and handed it to Petunia. "Happy birthday!"

"Thank you, Porky!" Petunia exclaimed. "It's just beautiful. It will remind me of a wonderful evening!"

And down the road they walked, with Bugs Bunny's carrots disappearing one after another—just like magic!